Birthday Balloons

Story by Beverley Randell
Illustrations by Abigail Marble

"Happy birthday, Tom," said Poppa.
"You are six, now,
and here are six balloons for you."

"Thanks, Poppa," said Tom.
"I love balloons."

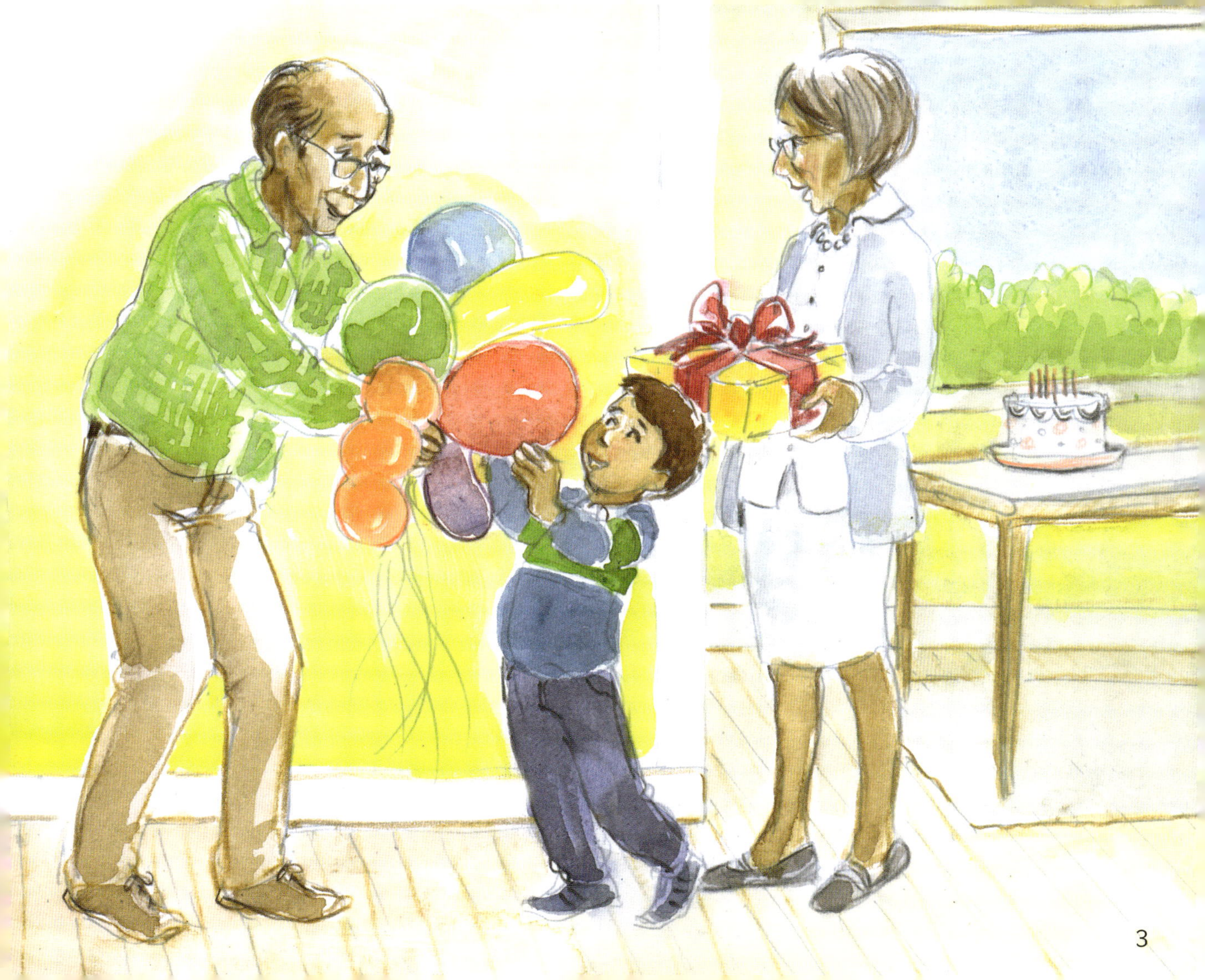

Baby Emma woke up.
She cried and cried.

"Here is your present, Tom," said Nana.

"Go on, Tom," said Mum.
"Open the box."

5

Tom opened the box.
He saw three little cars
and three little trucks.

"Oh, **thank** you," said Tom.

Emma went on crying.

7

Poppa and Tom had fun
playing with the cars and trucks.

"Come on, Emma. Come to Nana," said Nana.

But Emma went on crying.

"I can make her laugh," said Poppa, but Emma went on crying.

"Come here to me," said Mum,
but Emma went on crying.

Tom looked up at Emma.

"She is looking at my **balloons**," he said.

"I will get one for her."

13

"Here you are, Emma," said Tom.

"Here is a red balloon for you."

And Emma laughed!

"Thanks, Tom," said Mum.

"Emma is lucky to have a big brother like you!" said Dad.

15

Happy birthday to you,

Happy birthday to you,

Happy birthday dear Tom,

Happy birthday to you.